WHAT'S THE VERDICT?

YOU'RE THE JUDGE IN
90 TRICKY
COURTROOM QUIZZES

Ted LeValliant & Marcel Theroux
Illustrated by Myron Miller

 Sterling Publishing C

Library of Congress Cataloging-in-Publication Data

LeValliant, Ted.
    What's the verdict? : You're the Judge in 90 Tricky Courtroom Quizzes
/ Ted LeValliant & Marcel Theroux ; illustrated by Myron Miller.
        p.   cm.
    Includes index.
    ISBN 0-8069-7466-4 (paper)
    1. Justice, Administration of—United States—Problems, exercises,
etc.   2. Justice, Administration of—United States—Popular works.
3. Justice, Administration of—United States—Caricatures and
cartoons.   4. Judgments—United States—Problems, exercises, etc.
5. Judgments—United States—Popular works.   6. Judgments—United
States—Caricatures and cartoons.   I. Theroux, Marcel.   II. Title.
KF8700.Z95L48   1991
348.73'04—dc20
[347.3084]   90-28616
                                                                            CIP

10 9 8

© 1991 by Ted LeValliant and Marcel Theroux
Published by Sterling Publishing Company, Inc.
387 Park Avenue South, New York, N.Y. 10016
Distributed in Canada by Sterling Publishing
% Canadian Manda Group, P.O. Box 920, Station U
Toronto, Ontario, Canada M8Z 5P9
Distributed in Great Britain and Europe by Cassell PLC
Villiers House, 41/47 Strand, London WC2N 5JE, England
Distributed in Australia by Capricorn Ltd.
P.O. Box 665, Lane Cove, NSW 2066
Manufactured in the United States of America

Sterling ISBN 0-8069-7466-4   Paper

CONTENTS

HOW TO USE THIS BOOK

This is a book of legal puzzles, designed to exercise your mind and your reasoning powers.

First, you read the facts of a real-life court case. Then, you pit your judgment against that of the actual jury or trial judge. How do you think the case should have been decided? You can find out what really happened by looking up the "Trial Court Decision."

But was that the *right* decision? Every one of these cases has been appealed, so now you can match wits with the judges who reviewed them. Was the original decision upheld or overturned? Why? Look up the "Appeal Court Decision" and you'll find out.

If you keep statistics on your wins and losses, a pattern will emerge. How good a lawyer would you make?

* * * * * * * *

Note: The answers in the back of the book have been scrambled so that your crafty legal eye won't pick up the answer to the next case—by mistake.

* * * * * * * *

You can also play this book as a game. For the rules, see page 126.

PREFACE

This is not a work of fiction. It is a collection of real court cases taken from published reports. The cases come primarily from the United States. A few are from the United Kingdom and Canada. Most of the cases date from the last half of this century, although several are more than a hundred years old.

All the cases were the subjects of appeal to a higher court. This indicates that the point of law involved is difficult and caused reasonable jurists to disagree over the result. On appeal, many of the judgments were not unanimous; this further shows that the legal issues are not easy.

In addition, the cases are consistent with the general current of the law in the United States and in common law countries. This does not mean that a court hearing a particular case today would necessarily decide the case in the same way that it was decided before. It does mean, however, that the analysis of the court would proceed along the same lines and consider generally the same arguments. Having stated this qualification, we nevertheless believe that the vast majority of the cases in this book would probably be decided the same way today as they were when they were tried.

Throughout, the authors have also striven for uniformity of philosophy and approach. In other words, the results in the cases are not arbitrary. No decision in this book directly contradicts another. No reader will be frustrated because of lack of internal consistency within this book.

We have also made every attempt to avoid trick solutions to the cases. There are no rabbits pulled out of hats. Where we thought a legal principle was needed to decide a case, we summarized that principle for the reader.

Facts are always crucial to the resolution of a legal dispute. All the facts that you will need are laid out in the synopsis of the case. Don't be tempted to add new facts or to embellish existing ones. You will not be asked to decide, for example, whether a particular individual is telling the truth or not in a particular case. You can safely assume the truth of the facts and the assertions in the cases, unless you are asked to do otherwise in the question itself.

You, the reader, are actually being asked to do a dual job. First, you play the role of the jury. You are not expected to decide the facts, but rather to apply the law to the facts as they are set out. You are deciding concrete cases, just as a jury does. Then, you get a chance to sit in judgment of the jury and examine the trial decision. You then decide whether the legal principles are fair or justified or indeed logical.

You don't need to be a lawyer to enjoy this book or to get the "right" answers. In fact, some lawyers may be at a disadvantage. The process of legal reasoning is no different from that of any other type of reasoning. Care, common sense and imagination should lead to the correct solution in most cases, regardless of previous education or training.

The law is fascinating, particularly when it is stripped down to the essential issues of right and wrong, common sense and nonsense. Our experience has shown that the cases contained in these pages will stimulate, provoke and amuse you. We hope that you have fun with them.

QUESTIONS
OF LAW

The law states that "an assault is committed when a person unlawfully applies force to another person or creates in the mind of that other person a reasonable apprehension of the unlawful application of force."

1. The Lady and the Lecher

The unescorted young lady was walking down a road to go to work. The hopeful lecher drove by her very slowly and leered at her. He stopped his car, got out, and watched her until she was out of sight. The young lady was badly frightened by the experience.

Is the hopeful lecher guilty of assault?

TRIAL COURT DECISION: PAGE 100
APPEAL COURT DECISION: PAGE 108

2. A Fig By Any Other Name

Paul gave Jane a fig to eat. Paul had amorous intentions towards Jane. In order to encourage her, Paul put a drug (thought to be an aphrodisiac) into the fig. Jane became very ill, discovered the tampering with the fig, and now lays a charge of assault against Paul.

Is Paul guilty of assault?

TRIAL COURT DECISION: PAGE 102
APPEAL COURT DECISION: PAGE 110

3. Flash Fire

John negligently caused a flash fire in a restaurant. An employee activated an extinguisher, which caused a hissing sound. On hearing the sound, a customer shouted that gas was escaping and that there would be an explosion. The customers stampeded and Harry was injured in the stampede. Harry sued John for damages.

Does Harry succeed?

TRIAL COURT DECISION: PAGE 104
APPEAL COURT DECISION: PAGE 109

4. Cutthroat Law

Shortal spent the night at the house of his friends, the Blakelys. Upon returning from errands, the Blakelys found Shortal in the kitchen. Shortal had cut his throat. The Blakelys were both violently shocked and upset, and they sue Shortal's estate for damages for shock and nervousness.

Will the Blakelys succeed?

TRIAL COURT DECISION: PAGE 101
APPEAL COURT DECISION: PAGE 111

5. Many Are Called—Few Answer

Ron rented a canoe to Tim, who went out in it. The canoe overturned and Tim, now deceased, called for help. Ron heard the calls but ignored them. Tim's estate sues Ron.

Does Tim's estate recover?

TRIAL COURT DECISION: PAGE 103
APPEAL COURT DECISION: PAGE 112

A law states that "a private communication that has been intercepted is inadmissible as evidence against the originator of the communication, unless the originator or the person intended by the originator to receive it has expressly consented to the admission thereof."

6. Oh, God!

Victor was charged with arson. He was brought into a room where he was left alone. While being watched and taped, he got down on his knees and said: "Oh, God, let me get away with it just this once."

Is this conversation admissible in evidence?

TRIAL COURT DECISION: PAGE 105
APPEAL COURT DECISION: PAGE 114

7. The Sword or the Scalpel?

Louis stabbed the victim. The victim died of pneumonia because of negligent medical treatment of the stab wound. Louis was charged with murder.

Is Louis guilty of murder?

TRIAL COURT DECISION: PAGE 100
APPEAL COURT DECISION: PAGE 113

8. Taking the Law Into His Own Hands

Dean shot the victim (now deceased) in the abdomen. The wound was mortal and would have caused death within one hour, but before then the deceased slit his own throat. The throat wound would normally result in death after five minutes. Dean is charged with murder.

Is Dean guilty?

TRIAL COURT DECISION: PAGE 102
APPEAL COURT DECISION: PAGE 115

9. Pen Pals

The charge is murder. The defense is insanity. The defense tries to place in evidence letters written by the accused, while in a psychiatric hospital, to Pope Pius XII, the FBI, the Secret Service and Walter Winchell.

Are these letters admissible in evidence?

TRIAL COURT DECISION: PAGE 104
APPEAL COURT DECISION: PAGE 116

10. The Other Woman

Lucy sued for divorce. Her husband, Mac, also sued for divorce in the same lawsuit. Mac, however, refused to answer questions about his relationship with the "other woman." Mac's position is that he does not have to testify about his own wrongdoing because that would violate his privilege against self-incrimination.

Must Mac testify about the "other woman" if he wishes to pursue his suit for divorce?

TRIAL COURT DECISION: PAGE 101
APPEAL COURT DECISION: PAGE 118

11. The Naked Truth?

The police placed Edmund in a police lineup. They also seized physical evidence from Edmund, took his fingerprints, took his photograph while he was in custody, and required that Edmund remove his clothing for identification purposes.

Did the police in any way violate Edmund's privilege against self-incrimination?

TRIAL COURT DECISION: PAGE 103
APPEAL COURT DECISION: PAGE 117

12. Twice Cruel

Natalie sues for divorce. Can Natalie place in evidence the fact that her husband was divorced by a former wife for cruelty?

TRIAL COURT DECISION: PAGE 105
APPEAL COURT DECISION: PAGE 119

13. The Belligerent Victim

The defense is self-defense. Dennis, the accused, seeks to show that the deceased had a reputation for violence. Dennis argues that this evidence would show that the deceased, more likely than not, was the first aggressor.

Is the evidence admissible?

TRIAL COURT DECISION: PAGE 100
APPEAL COURT DECISION: PAGE 120

14. The Case of the Slippery Floor

Marsha fell on a terrazzo floor rendered slippery by rain. The defense seeks to show that no complaint about anyone slipping had been received during fifteen years though 4,000 to 5,000 people entered the store every day.

Can the defense show this?

TRIAL COURT DECISION: PAGE 102
APPEAL COURT DECISION: PAGE 122

15. Shocking Pictures

In a criminal trial, pictures of the victim are tendered as evidence. The defense objects because the pictures are shocking and therefore might inflame the jury.

Are the pictures admissible?

TRIAL COURT DECISION: PAGE 104
APPEAL COURT DECISION: PAGE 124

16. Stabbed and Twice Dropped

Mildred stabbed the victim. The victim was transported to the hospital. The victim was twice dropped by the person carrying him. The hospital had no facilities for blood transfusions. Had the victim received blood, he would have had a 75 percent chance of survival. Mildred is charged with murder.

Is Mildred guilty?

TRIAL COURT DECISION: PAGE 101
APPEAL COURT DECISION: PAGE 121

17. Buying Votes?

The jury was allowed outside the courtroom to view the scene of the accident. After the view, one of the people involved in the lawsuit entertained the jury in a local saloon. The other side in the case discovered this and asked for a mistrial.

Did the court order a mistrial?

TRIAL COURT DECISION: PAGE 103
APPEAL COURT DECISION: PAGE 123

18. Serendipity in the Third

Police raided a bookie joint. During the raid, a phone call is taken by an officer. The caller says: "Put $100 on Serendipity in the third." At the trial, the prosecution tries to put this call in evidence. The defense objects and alleges that it is hearsay.

Is the evidence admissible?

TRIAL COURT DECISION: PAGE 105
APPEAL COURT DECISION: PAGE 125

19. A Bad Reference

Employers are generally liable for the negligence of their employees. Otto, an employer, is sued by Jane for injuries Jane sustained as the result of Floyd's negligence. Floyd is an employee of Otto. Jane proposes to call witnesses to testify that Otto's foreman had complained before the accident of Floyd's incompetence. Otto claims that the complaints are hearsay.

Is the evidence admissible?

TRIAL COURT DECISION: PAGE 100
APPEAL COURT DECISION: PAGE 108

20. The Unsuccessful Pickpocket

Connie put her hand in the victim's pocket. The victim grabbed Connie's wrist while her hand was in the pocket. The charge is attempted theft. There was no money in the pocket.

Is Connie guilty?

TRIAL COURT DECISION: PAGE 102
APPEAL COURT DECISION: PAGE 110

21. Fear of Fleeing

The charge is murder. The prosecution wants to show that, at a time after the murder, the accused, Polly, was arrested for reckless driving. Polly attempted to bribe the arresting officer and eventually she escaped. The defense argues that this evidence is not relevant to the murder charge.

Is the evidence admissible?

TRIAL COURT DECISION: PAGE 104
APPEAL COURT DECISION: PAGE 109

22. The Employer's Wrath

A newspaper is sued for libel. The victim of the libel wants to prove that the newspaper fired the reporter who wrote the story shortly after it appeared. The lawyer for the newspaper claims that this should be inadmissible on the grounds that it is not relevant.

Is the evidence of the firing admissible?

TRIAL COURT DECISION: PAGE 101
APPEAL COURT DECISION: PAGE 111

23. Her Husband Did It

In a murder trial, a witness called by the prosecution will testify that the victim (the wife of the physician-defendant) had said to a nurse, "My husband has poisoned me."

Is this statement admissible?

TRIAL COURT DECISION: PAGE 103
APPEAL COURT DECISION: PAGE 112

24. Stop the Bus!

In a trial resulting from a collision between a bus and another vehicle, the victim calls a witness who was a passenger on the bus. The witness will say that the driver exclaimed, just before the collision, "I have no brakes." The defense lawyer claims that this statement is inadmissible as hearsay.

Is the statement admissible?

TRIAL COURT DECISION: PAGE 105
APPEAL COURT DECISION: PAGE 114

25. Possession of a Firearm

Darlene was charged under two separate laws with possession of a firearm. The possible sentences under each law were different, but the facts necessary to support a conviction were the same.

Can Darlene be charged with and convicted of both offenses?

TRIAL COURT DECISION: PAGE 100
APPEAL COURT DECISION: PAGE 113

26. Armed Robbery

Leander was charged with armed robbery and with using a firearm to commit an offense. Both charges arose out of the same robbery.

Can Leander be tried and convicted of both offenses?

TRIAL COURT DECISION: PAGE 102
APPEAL COURT DECISION: PAGE 115

27. Speedy Trial

An accused is entitled to a speedy trial. Roxane was acquitted because the prosecution took too long to bring the case to trial. Can Roxane be tried again for the same offense?

TRIAL COURT DECISION: PAGE 104
APPEAL COURT DECISION: PAGE 116

28. Expensive Upgrade

Cedric leased a parcel of land to Montgomery. Montgomery was allowed to carry away sand and gravel, but he was required to leave the land at a uniform grade. Montgomery left the land at an uneven grade. It will cost $100,000 to grade the land properly. The land, however, is only worth $25,000 when properly graded.

Can Cedric recover the $100,000 from Montgomery to grade the land?

TRIAL COURT DECISION: PAGE 101
APPEAL COURT DECISION: PAGE 118

29. A Misfire

Alan's barn caught fire. Alan called the police inspector and asked for a fire truck. The inspector phoned the wrong fire station, one outside the jurisdiction in which Alan's barn was located. The station sent a truck. Everyone thought the fire station was inside the proper jurisdiction, but it wasn't. There is a fee for fighting fires outside the jurisdiction of the fire station, so the fire station sent Alan a bill for services rendered.

Does Alan have to pay despite the common error?

TRIAL COURT DECISION: PAGE 103
APPEAL COURT DECISION: PAGE 117

30. The Right Charge

Eunice switched price tags on an article of clothing. She proceeded to the check-out counter and paid the price indicated on the switched tag. Eunice was later arrested and charged with theft. The defense argues that this was not a theft but rather a fraud, since Eunice had concluded a contract for the purchase of the article but under false pretenses.

Is Eunice guilty of theft?

TRIAL COURT DECISION: PAGE 105
APPEAL COURT DECISION: PAGE 119

31. Hair Today and Tomorrow

A hair removal clinic offered to permanently remove facial hair. It advertises that the results are guaranteed. In response to the ads, Shirley went to the clinic and paid for the treatment. Shirley's hair loss was not permanent and she sued for breach of contract.

Did Shirley win?

TRIAL COURT DECISION: PAGE 100
APPEAL COURT DECISION: PAGE 120

32. The Tired Lawyer

Rose was represented by a very tired lawyer. Indeed, the lawyer slept through a substantial portion of Rose's trial. Rose was found guilty. Rose appealed. Rose could not, however, point to any actual harm to her case because of her lawyer's naps.

Should Rose's appeal be allowed?

TRIAL COURT DECISION: PAGE 102
APPEAL COURT DECISION: PAGE 122

Child neglect is defined as "leaving, with criminal negligence, a child unattended in or at any place for such period of time as may be likely to endanger the health or welfare of such child." The words "criminal negligence" mean that "a person fails to be aware of substantial and unjustifiable risk that the result will occur or that the circumstance exists."

33. Child Neglect?

Isabel had two children, aged eight and twenty-two months. She left the children alone to go to a party at a local tavern. While she was away, the children were killed in a fire, the cause of which is unknown. Isabel is charged with child neglect.

   Is she guilty?

TRIAL COURT DECISION: PAGE 104
APPEAL COURT DECISION: PAGE 124

34. Unwarranted Measures?

The police obtained a search warrant in the belief that Morton
had heroin in his possession. Morton's door had an outer iron
gate that could be left locked until Morton decided whether to
let a caller in. The police were afraid that if they told Morton
about the warrant, he might leave the gate locked and destroy
the evidence. To avoid this, they forged an arrest warrant on
fictitious traffic offenses and showed it to Morton. Morton let
the police in to clear up the "mistake." Then they showed him
the search warrant and found heroin. Morton is charged with
possession of heroin. He argues that the search was illegal.

Is Morton found guilty?

TRIAL COURT DECISION: PAGE 101
APPEAL COURT DECISION: PAGE 121

41

35. Leader of the Pact

Alex and Brett were unhappy youths. They made a suicide pact. To carry out the pact, Alex drove his car over a cliff, with Brett as his passenger. Brett died. Alex recovered. Alex is charged with murder.

Is Alex guilty?

TRIAL COURT DECISION: PAGE 103
APPEAL COURT DECISION: PAGE 123

A law concerning "ambulance-chasing" provides that it is an offense for a lawyer to solicit a person who has been injured in an accident, if the soliciting is for the purpose of commencing legal proceedings for that person.

36. Ambulance-Chasing

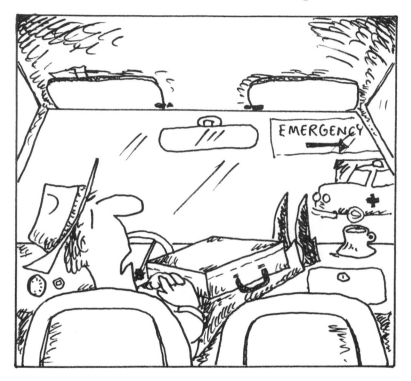

Fabian heard that Mr. Jones had been injured in an accident. He thought that Jones had a good negligence case, and talked to him about starting a lawsuit. Fabian is charged under the law and argues that the law is invalid because it is too broad and because it prohibits freedom of speech.

Is Fabian guilty?

TRIAL COURT DECISION: PAGE 105
APPEAL COURT DECISION: PAGE 125

37. Caution—Inflammable!

Larry, an engineer, decided to apply a floor sealer in his recreation room. He did not extinguish the pilot light on his gas furnace in the adjacent room. It caused an explosion when the vapors from the sealer came in contact with it. Larry was seriously injured and sued the manufacturer of the sealer for negligence because the warning on the sealer stated only "Keep Away From Fire, Heat and Open-Flame Lights" and "Caution Inflammable! Keep Away From Open Flame!"

Is Larry's lawsuit successful?

TRIAL COURT DECISION: PAGE 100
APPEAL COURT DECISION: PAGE 108

38. "This *Is* a Constable, Constable"

Curtis purchased a painting at a well-known art gallery. The painting was by the artist Constable. Five years later, Curtis discovered that the painting was not by Constable.

Can Curtis get his money back?

TRIAL COURT DECISION: PAGE 102
APPEAL COURT DECISION: PAGE 110

39. Off-Duty?

A police officer was working, while off-duty, at a rock concert. He was in uniform and was working with the knowledge and consent of his superiors but was being paid by the concert promoters. Richmond assaulted the police officer and was charged with assaulting an officer. Richmond argues that he did not assault someone who was working as an officer but only a private security guard.

Is Richmond guilty?

TRIAL COURT DECISION: PAGE 104
APPEAL COURT DECISION: PAGE 109

40. Sealed Bag

A government informer contacted John, informing him that cocaine was available for purchase. John said that he had $22,000 and that he would meet with the informer the next day. When John met with the informer, an undercover police officer was present. The officer took John to a nearby hotel room where John asked to see the cocaine. The officer left the room and returned with a sealed bag. The officer refused to open the bag, but John would only produce his money if the bag were opened. They argued for several minutes and John left. He was arrested shortly thereafter and charged with attempting to possess cocaine with the intent to distribute.

Is John guilty?

TRIAL COURT DECISION: PAGE 101
APPEAL COURT DECISION: PAGE 111

41. Tavern License

Wally was a waiter in a tavern. He served alcohol to a minor, contrary to law. Wally entered into plea negotiations and agreed to plead guilty in return for the state agreeing "that it will not take further action by way of hearing before any court, or agency for action arising out of this transaction." After Wally's plea and conviction, Wally's employer, the owner of the tavern, was notified of a hearing before the local liquor licensing board to consider revocation of his tavern owner's license. The tavern owner argues that the state cannot revoke his license because of its agreement with Wally.

Can the tavern owner's license be revoked?

TRIAL COURT DECISION: PAGE 103
APPEAL COURT DECISION: PAGE 112

42. Burgled Burglar?

Alfredo was charged with burglary. A witness who chased him testified that the thief was wearing a white tee shirt with an emblem on the back, blue jeans and tennis shoes, and that he ran across a patch of red gravel. When Alfredo was booked, the police placed his clothes in a personal property bag. At the trial, Alfredo asked that his clothing be produced, in order to show that he was not the thief. When the bag was opened, no shoes or pants were found. Alfredo asks that the charge be dismissed on the basis that important evidence has been lost by the prosecution.

Should the charge be dismissed?

TRIAL COURT DECISION: PAGE 105
APPEAL COURT DECISION: PAGE 114

A law provides that certain communications between social workers and their clients are privileged and can therefore not be disclosed. The privilege applies to information given to the social worker "in his professional capacity that was necessary to enable him to render services in his professional capacity."

43. Dial M for Murder

Herbert is charged with murder. At 5:00 A.M., he phoned a psychiatric social worker with whom he had consulted on several prior occasions. Herbert told the social worker that he had just killed someone, and that he understood that the police would have to be notified. Herbert then gave his address.

Is the telephone conversation privileged within the meaning of the law?

TRIAL COURT DECISION: PAGE 100
APPEAL COURT DECISION: PAGE 113

44. Discount Theft?

Timothy stole four men's suits. He is charged with theft over $200.00. The only evidence of the value of the suits was given by the security guard who arrested Timothy. The guard admitted that he got the price of the suits from the price tags, which indicated a price of $300.00.

Is Timothy guilty of theft over $200.00?

TRIAL COURT DECISION: PAGE 102
APPEAL COURT DECISION: PAGE 115

45. Rapid Fire

Linda was shot three times. A witness heard the shots, went to help Linda and reached her within seconds of the shooting. The witness asked Linda who shot her and Linda replied that Carol had shot her. Carol is charged with murder.

Can the witness testify as to what Linda told him?

TRIAL COURT DECISION: PAGE 104
APPEAL COURT DECISION: PAGE 116

A defendant is entitled to be presumed innocent until proven guilty.

46. Not Presumed Innocent

A prosecutor made the following comments in front of a jury: "You are to go through the trial with the presumption of innocence, and you should retain that attitude up through that point. But once you walk into that jury room you no longer have that responsibility—that mantle of the presumption of innocence; once you get into that jury room you no longer have to leave that mantle about his shoulders. You have the right to take it off."

Is the above statement sufficient to result in a mistrial?

TRIAL COURT DECISION: PAGE 101
APPEAL COURT DECISION: PAGE 118

47. Double Dose of Cyanide

Henry was a goldsmith. He used potassium cyanide in his trade. Henry's wife died of potassium cyanide poisoning. Henry is charged with the murder of his wife. At his trial, the prosecution wants to show that Henry's previous wife had died, three years earlier, of potassium cyanide poisoning. Henry objects, claiming that this evidence would unfairly prejudice him in the eyes of the jury. There is no direct evidence that Henry administered the poison to either wife.

Is the evidence of the earlier poisoning admissible?

TRIAL COURT DECISION: PAGE 103
APPEAL COURT DECISION: PAGE 117

Before a confession can be admitted as evidence, the prosecution must show that it has been given freely and voluntarily, without fear of threat or violence.

48. The Ends Justify the Means?

Jake kidnapped a young girl. He was arrested while trying to collect the ransom. Jake's accomplice was apparently holding the young girl at gunpoint and the police were most anxious to discover her location. The police choked Jake, twisted his arm behind his back and physically abused him until he revealed the girl's whereabouts. After Jake told the police where the girl was, he gave them a complete confession. The prosecution seeks to put the confession in evidence but the defense argues that Jake's confession was involuntary because of the violence used by the police.

Is Jake's confession admissible?

TRIAL COURT DECISION: PAGE 105
APPEAL COURT DECISION: PAGE 119

49. Unfaded Memory

An elderly married couple was met in their dining room by a man holding a hatchet. The man struck them, robbed, bound and gagged them. That same evening, each member of the couple independently viewed six photographs. They each identified Mario as the robber. At the trial, however, neither the husband nor the wife could identify Mario in person. The prosecution relied on the fact that they had identified Mario by means of photographs.

Is this evidence sufficient to convict Mario of the offense?

TRIAL COURT DECISION: PAGE 100
APPEAL COURT DECISION: PAGE 120

50. You Can Rely on Us

The accountants prepared financial statements for a client so that he could obtain financing from the bank. The accountants were negligent in the preparation of the statements. The bank had no relationship with the accountants, but the bank relied on the statements. The client went bankrupt. The bank sues the accountants.

Does the bank succeed?

TRIAL COURT DECISION: PAGE 102
APPEAL COURT DECISION: PAGE 122

The law provides that a person is guilty of robbery in the first degree if that person "attempts to kill anyone or purposely inflicts or attempts to inflict serious bodily harm, or is armed with or uses or threatens the immediate use of a deadly weapon."

51. Less Than Meets the Eye

Jim robbed a woman in a parking lot. He had his hand in his coat pocket and pretended that he was concealing a revolver. The woman believed that Jim had a revolver, but Jim in fact had none. Jim is charged with robbery in the first degree.

Is he guilty of robbery in the first degree?

TRIAL COURT DECISION: PAGE 104
APPEAL COURT DECISION: PAGE 124

52. Convenience Store Mugging

Alice went shopping at a convenience store operated by the Acme Corporation. Alice was mugged in the well-lighted parking lot and sustained injuries. In the year preceding Alice's mugging, seven other muggings had occurred in the parking lot of the same store. Acme hired a security guard, but he was inside the store when Alice was assaulted. Alice sues Acme for failure to warn and for failure to provide adequate security.

Is Alice successful?

TRIAL COURT DECISION: PAGE 101
APPEAL COURT DECISION: PAGE 121

53. Policing the Police

Alphonse, a police officer, was required by the Police Department to carry his gun at all times within city limits. He returned home one day, shot his wife and committed suicide. The wife suffered brain damage and now sues the Police Department for negligence. The wife argues that the Police Department failed to adopt an effective program of psychological screening of police officers. The Department had tried several psychological programs in an effort to screen out emotionally unstable officers, but these had proven ineffective and had been abandoned.

Is the Police Department guilty of negligence?

TRIAL COURT DECISION: PAGE 103
APPEAL COURT DECISION: PAGE 123

54. Unfinished Business

Boris and Charlie were caught behind a liquor store during the early morning hours. Boris and Charlie had broken approximately halfway through the store's rear wall. They are charged with breaking and entering with intent to steal.

Are they guilty?

TRIAL COURT DECISION: PAGE 105
APPEAL COURT DECISION: PAGE 125

55. Kidnapping Jenny's Daughter

Michael conspired with an accomplice, Jenny, to take her daughter from a child welfare agency. Jenny took the child from the agency at gunpoint. Michael is charged with conspiring to kidnap the child. The law provides that a parent cannot be convicted of kidnapping her child. Michael is not a parent.

Is Michael guilty?

TRIAL COURT DECISION: PAGE 100
APPEAL COURT DECISION: PAGE 108

56. The Wrong Parts

Harold was employed by an airline and had the authority to order parts. He bought and caused to be delivered car parts that could not be used by the airline but could be used on his own car. Other employees of the airline owned the same make of car as Harold. Harold is charged with embezzling automobile parts.

Is Harold guilty?

TRIAL COURT DECISION: PAGE 102
APPEAL COURT DECISION: PAGE 110

57. A Gift of Hacksaw Blades

Gerrard was a prison inmate. His devoted girlfriend, Dawn, visited him. She was anxious to see him free and, in order to help him escape, passed him four hacksaw blades. An attentive guard saw Dawn pass Gerrard the blades, and after a search, seized them. Gerrard is charged with attempted escape.

Is Gerrard guilty?

TRIAL COURT DECISION: PAGE 104
APPEAL COURT DECISION: PAGE 109

58. The Defense of Diligence

Peter abandoned his wife and children. The wife worked two jobs and was aided by her family and local church. Both the wife and children had adequate food and shelter. Peter made no payments to the wife. He is charged with criminal non-support of his children. In order for the prosecution to gain a conviction, it must show that the children were in "necessitous circumstances" at the relevant time.

Is Peter guilty?

TRIAL COURT DECISION: PAGE 101
APPEAL COURT DECISION: PAGE 111

59. Too Late for Pistol-Packing

Sally wanted to bring her revolver with her to New York. She had a New York license to carry the pistol. Sally arrived at the Chicago airport but she was too late to check the suitcase that contained her revolver. She was told to go to the gate with her luggage. As Sally went through the x-ray machine, the alarm went off and the gun was discovered.

Is Sally guilty of attempting to board an aircraft while having a gun in her possession?

TRIAL COURT DECISION: PAGE 103
APPEAL COURT DECISION: PAGE 112

60. The Joke's on You!

Morris had been drinking when he entered the bank. "I have a .38 in my pocket," he said to the teller, "and I want all your money." The teller set off a silent alarm. But when she handed Morris the cash, he said he had been joking all along. He left the bank empty-handed and was arrested.

Is Morris guilty of attempted robbery?

TRIAL COURT DECISION: PAGE 105
APPEAL COURT DECISION: PAGE 114

61. Choose Your Weapon Carefully

Alexander robbed a store while armed with a B-B gun. The B-B gun looked like a .45 caliber semi-automatic pistol but fired B-Bs by means of a spring. Alexander is charged with using a firearm in the commission of a criminal offense. The word "firearm" is not defined in the law. Alexander argues that "firearm" should be defined as a weapon that fires a projectile by means of gunpowder.

Is Alexander guilty?

TRIAL COURT DECISION: PAGE 100
APPEAL COURT DECISION: PAGE 113

62. Intoxication Plus

Ralph killed a bicycle rider while driving his truck. There was no evidence that Ralph's driving was noticeably bad. Ralph's blood test however indicated that he had a blood-alcohol level of .16%. The law provided that a .10% blood-alcohol level was evidence of intoxication, absent proof to the contrary.

Can Ralph be convicted of causing death by criminal negligence?

TRIAL COURT DECISION: PAGE 102
APPEAL COURT DECISION: PAGE 115

63. Practical Joker

Morris was the mischievous sort. As a practical joke, he bent a stop sign at an intersection. Bill was driving through the intersection, could not see the stop sign, and collided with Colleen's car. Colleen was killed in the crash. Morris is charged with negligent homicide.

Is Morris guilty?

TRIAL COURT DECISION: PAGE 104
APPEAL COURT DECISION: PAGE 116

64. Take the Money and Run

An insurance company paid a widow money under an insurance policy on her husband's life. They did so by mistake, since the policy had lapsed for non-payment of premiums.

Can the widow keep the money?

TRIAL COURT DECISION: PAGE 101
APPEAL COURT DECISION: PAGE 118

65. The Fatal Hostage

Steve and Tim took Caroline hostage while attempting to escape from an armed robbery. The police arrived and during a pitched battle with Steve and Tim, Caroline was shot and killed by the police. Steve and Tim are charged with the "felony murder" of Caroline. They argue that they cannot be held responsible for the death of Caroline since the police caused the death of Caroline, not Steve or Tim.

Are they guilty of murder?

TRIAL COURT DECISION: PAGE 103
APPEAL COURT DECISION: PAGE 117

66. She Never Heard of Henry

Henry never paid his traffic tickets. There were several warrants outstanding against him. One day, Henry's car was parked in front of Kate's house. Police knocked at Kate's door and asked for Henry. Kate said that she had never heard of him. Undeterred, the police looked through a window and saw Henry hiding in the basement. They arrested him. Kate is charged with hampering or impeding a public official in the performance of his lawful duties?

Is Kate guilty?

TRIAL COURT DECISION: PAGE 105
APPEAL COURT DECISION: PAGE 119

Under the law relating to "criminal simulation" an offense is committed if an object is made or altered so as to have an appearance of "antiquity, rarity, source, or authorship" that it does not in fact have.

67. Mass Produced

Avery sold Bryce a one-jewel watch that had a famous trademark on it. Avery told Bryce that the watch was a genuine seventeen-jewel watch when in fact it was not. Avery is charged with "criminal simulation."

Is he guilty of the offense?

TRIAL COURT DECISION: PAGE 100
APPEAL COURT DECISION: PAGE 120

68. Cruise Control

Pierre had to drive long distances because of his work. He liked to use the automatic cruise control. He set the control at the speed limit but was nevertheless ticketed for speeding. At his trial, he showed that the automatic cruise control had malfunctioned on the day in question.

Is Pierre guilty of speeding?

TRIAL COURT DECISION: PAGE 102
APPEAL COURT DECISION: PAGE 122

69. Once or Forever?

Daniel was a police officer. One day he decided to keep a coat that he knew had been stolen. Thirteen months later he was charged with improper conduct in office. There is no doubt that receipt of the stolen coat was improper conduct in office. But a prosecution for such an offense must begin less than twelve months after the alleged crime. The prosecution argues that possession of the coat by Daniel was a continuing offense committed every day during the thirteen months, and that therefore the twelve month statute of limitations had not expired. But the defense argues that the prosecution was begun too late.

Is Daniel guilty?

TRIAL COURT DECISION: PAGE 104
APPEAL COURT DECISION: PAGE 124

70. Murder, She Said

Abigail and Barney were cut-throat competitors. Unable to eliminate a business rival by legitimate means, they decided to have him killed. Abigail flew to New York and met with an undercover police officer. Abigail offered the officer $2,500.00 to murder the rival. The officer agreed and Abigail said that she would mail him the rival's photograph, a map of his cottage and the fee. Several days later, Abigail called off the murder.

Is Abigail guilty of conspiracy to commit murder?

TRIAL COURT DECISION: PAGE 101
APPEAL COURT DECISION: PAGE 121

71. Illegal Search?

Earl grew marijuana on his farm. Narcotics agents drove to Earl's farm, passed his house, and came upon a locked gate with a "no trespassing" sign. The agents used a footpath to walk around the gate and found a field of marijuana about one mile from Earl's house. The agents had no warrant. Earl is charged with cultivating marijuana and argues that the search is illegal.

Is the evidence admissible?

TRIAL COURT DECISION: PAGE 103
APPEAL COURT DECISION: PAGE 123

72. On-the-Job Training

Lloyd was charged with a complicated mail fraud. His lawyer withdrew just before the trial and the court appointed a young lawyer with a real estate practice to defend Lloyd. The lawyer had never handled a jury trial and was allowed only twenty-five days to prepare, although the prosecution had taken four and a half years to investigate the case. Lloyd is convicted and appeals on the basis that his lawyer was young, inexperienced and had been given too little time to prepare, given the complexity of the case.

Is Lloyd's appeal successful?

TRIAL COURT DECISION: PAGE 105
APPEAL COURT DECISION: PAGE 125

73. The Lawyer Was Wrong

Oliver was charged with a criminal offense. The penalty for the offense was fixed by law to a period of ten years. Oliver's lawyer told him that he would be entitled to parole after three years. On the basis of this advice, Oliver pleaded guilty. Unfortunately, his lawyer had been wrong about the parole. Oliver was only eligible for parole after seven years. Oliver was understandably quite perturbed and he now seeks to change his plea and be awarded a new trial.

Is Oliver entitled to a new trial?

TRIAL COURT DECISION: PAGE 100
APPEAL COURT DECISION: PAGE 108

74. The Accompanist

Munroe was the manager of a popular singer. Munroe thought that Glen, a pianist, had agreed to accompany the singer at a forthcoming concert. Munroe issued posters and programs that showed Glen as pianist for the singer's performance. In fact, Glen had not agreed to accompany the singer. As a result of the posters, Glen lost another contract, because people believed that Glen was unavailable.

Can Glen recover damages because of the statements in the poster?

TRIAL COURT DECISION: PAGE 102
APPEAL COURT DECISION: PAGE 110

75. Inlaw Outlaw

Debby was a two-year old infant. Philamena was Debby's aunt-in-law (the widow of a brother of Debby's mother). Philamena obtained insurance on Debby's life from an insurance company. Philamena named herself beneficiary. The insurance company should not have issued the policy to Philamena, because Philamena had no "insurable interest" in the life of Debby (Debby and Philamena were not closely enough related). Philamena murdered Debby in order to collect on the insurance policy. Debby's father sues the insurance company for negligently issuing the policy to Philamena.

Should Debby's father be successful?

TRIAL COURT DECISION: PAGE 104
APPEAL COURT DECISION: PAGE 109

76. Water Works

During construction work, Albert negligently broke a street water main causing a loss in water pressure. The city was very slow in repairing the main and, after a time when repairs ought to have been made by the city, Pierre's house caught on fire. Pierre's house burned down because of the low water pressure.

Can Pierre successfully sue Albert?

TRIAL COURT DECISION: PAGE 101
APPEAL COURT DECISION: PAGE 111

A criminal statute defines the offense of perjury as follows: "Every one commits perjury who, being a witness in a judicial proceeding, with intent to mislead gives false evidence, knowing that the evidence is false."

77. No Harm, No Foul?

Marcel lied on the stand with intent to mislead. The trial court disregarded Marcel's evidence which did not figure in its verdict. Marcel is charged with perjury.

Is Marcel guilty?

TRIAL COURT DECISION: PAGE 103
APPEAL COURT DECISION: PAGE 112

78. The Distracted Mother

Mary was a distracted mother. She did not carefully supervise her four-year-old son, Kerr. Kerr ran out from between parked cars and was struck by Gustave. The court appointed a guardian for Kerr. The guardian sues both Mary and Gustave for negligence.

Is Mary responsible in damage for negligently supervising Kerr?

TRIAL COURT DECISION: PAGE 105
APPEAL COURT DECISION: PAGE 114

79. Horse Sense

Nicole accused Reginald of acts of cruelty to a horse, including beating the horse and knocking out an eye. Reginald accused Nicole of slander. At the trial, Nicole showed that Reginald had in fact been cruel to the horse, but could not show that the horse's eye had been knocked out.

Is Reginald entitled to damages for slander?

TRIAL COURT DECISION: PAGE 100
APPEAL COURT DECISION: PAGE 113

80. Fool's Gold

Duncan was a kind soul, but not very clever. A fortune teller told him that a pot of gold could be found on his land. Ned, a practical joker, buried a pot on Duncan's land which he "discovered" in Duncan's presence. Duncan took the pot to the local bank and opened it, in front of a howling, jeering crowd. Duncan suffered deep mental suffering and humiliation.

Can Duncan recover damages from Ned?

TRIAL COURT DECISION: PAGE 102
APPEAL COURT DECISION: PAGE 115

*The constitution of the United States provides freedom of
speech and freedom of the press. But the law also provides
the right to be free from defamatory attacks against a person's reputation. What happens when these freedoms come
into conflict?*

81. Sign of the *Times*

Steve was an elected commissioner of the city of Montgomery,
Alabama. Steve was responsible for supervising the police department. Lowell was a black clergyman who paid for an ad in
the *New York Times* that accused Steve of persecuting civil
rights activists in Alabama. The ad contained several inac-
curacies of fact and Steve sued for defamation. The *Times* had
printed the ad, without checking its accuracy, on the strength
of Lowell's reputation.

Was Steve successful?

TRIAL COURT DECISION: PAGE 104
APPEAL COURT DECISION: PAGE 116

82. Bad Publicity

Millie was a wealthy socialite married to Johnny. Millie sued Johnny for divorce. The divorce trial was messy and very public. Evidence was led of extramarital activity on both sides, but the judge discounted much of it. *Hour* magazine carelessly got its facts wrong. In its "Milestones" column, it wrote the divorce had been granted on "grounds of extreme cruelty and adultery ... The seventeen-month intermittent trial produced enough testimony of extramarital adventures on both sides, said the judge, to make Dr. Freud's hair curl." Millie sues *Hour* magazine, which alleges that Millie was a public figure and that it is not liable for defamation in the absence of evidence of actual malice.

Should Millie be successful in her action for defamation?

TRIAL COURT DECISION: PAGE 101
APPEAL COURT DECISION: PAGE 118

The law provides that: "One who gives publicity to matters concerning the private life of another, of a kind highly offensive to a reasonable man, is subject to liability to the other for invasion of his privacy."

83. Invasion of Privacy?

Val was something of a spendthrift. His credit card was always over the limit. The credit card company became fed up and sent Val's account to the collection agency. The collection agency was aggressive. It telephoned Val's relatives. It wrote to Val's employer. The collection agency was not offensive, but it did discuss Val's debt with the person that it contacted.

Can Val recover damages for invasion of privacy?

TRIAL COURT DECISION: PAGE 103
APPEAL COURT DECISION: PAGE 117

In an insurance policy insuring against death by "external, violent and accidental means," the means of death must generally be accidental and independent of all other causes. While it is not always easy to determine whether a person has died by external, violent and accidental means, this determination is crucial to recovery under many life insurance policies.

84. The Fatal Trip

Abe was a chronic alcoholic. On his first day in the hospital, he had a convulsion while en route to the bathroom. He struck his head and died. Abe's trip to the bathroom was unsupervised by hospital staff.

Did Abe die by external, violent and accidental means?

TRIAL COURT DECISION: PAGE 105
APPEAL COURT DECISION: PAGE 119

85. Blood Rights

Delores, 22 and unmarried, was severely injured in a car accident. She was taken unconscious to a nearby hospital, badly needing a blood transfusion. Delores and her parents were Jehovah's Witnesses. The parents refused to consent to the transfusion. The hospital authorities go before a judge in order to obtain permission to give Delores a transfusion.

Can the judge authorize the transfusion?

TRIAL COURT DECISION: PAGE 100
APPEAL COURT DECISION: PAGE 120

86. Tennis, Anyone?

Renee was a tennis player. She had played professional tennis as a male but, following a sex-change operation, she began to play as a female. Renee was very successful as a female tennis player. She wanted to play as a woman in the U.S. Open tournament. The tournament organizers decided to institute a chromosome test as a requirement for play. Renee could not, of course, pass this test even though she had all the sexual characteristics of a woman with the exception of the ability to bear children. Renee claims that the chromosome test violates her civil rights and that she should be considered a female. Renee seeks an injunction against the tournament organizers.

Should Renee be allowed to play?

TRIAL COURT DECISION: PAGE 102
APPEAL COURT DECISION: PAGE 122

87. A Matter of Faith

Igor applied to the university. Before acceptance, the university required a vaccination. Igor refused. The university supplied Igor with a printed form that allowed an exemption from vaccination on religious grounds. The form required a statement that the person seeking the exemption was a member of the Christian Science faith. Igor was not a Christian Scientist, but nevertheless objected to the vaccination on religious grounds. The university turned down Igor's application because he refused vaccination. Igor sued.

Should Igor be admitted to the university?

TRIAL COURT DECISION: PAGE 104
APPEAL COURT DECISION: PAGE 124

88. Home Cooking

Cynthia is charged with the murder of her husband by arsenic poisoning. There is no direct evidence against Cynthia. Cynthia, the husband, and their three sons lived together in the same house. Cynthia prepared their food and made tea for them. The prosecution seeks to prove that, after the husband's death, two sons died by arsenic poisoning and that the third became severely ill.

Can the prosecution place in evidence the death of the two sons?

TRIAL COURT DECISION: PAGE 101
APPEAL COURT DECISION: PAGE 121

89. Cost Cutting

In response to the explosion of medical malpractice claims, a law was passed limiting recovery in court cases for malpractice to $500,000. Cora, a four-year-old child, was badly injured by a doctor's negligence. Cora's guardian sues for $2,000,000 and argues that the law limiting damages is invalid.

Is the law valid?

TRIAL COURT DECISION: PAGE 103
APPEAL COURT DECISION: PAGE 123

90. The Good News and the Bad News

Utility Insurance Company employed Dr. Smith to examine Irving, an applicant for insurance. Irving badly needed insurance, but was very sick. Irving conspired with Dr. Smith to submit a false medical report. Utility granted insurance to Irving on the basis of the false report. Irving died soon after and Utility paid his beneficiaries. Some time later, Utility discovered the fraud and sued Dr. Smith and Dr. Smith's medical malpractice insurer. The insurer was responsible for the doctor's "malpractice" and his "errors or mistakes."

Can Utility recover from Dr. Smith's insurer?

TRIAL COURT DECISION: PAGE 105
APPEAL COURT DECISION: PAGE 125

TRIAL COURT
DECISIONS

1. **The Lady and the Lecher**
   The hopeful lecher is guilty of assault.

7. **The Sword or the Scalpel?**
   Louis is guilty of murder.

13. **The Belligerent Victim**
    The evidence is admissible.

19. **A Bad Reference**
    The evidence is admissible.

25. **Possession of a Firearm**
    Darlene can be charged with and convicted of both offenses.

31. **Hair Today and Tomorrow**
    Shirley did not win.

37. **Caution—Inflammable!**
    Larry's suit is successful.

43. **Dial M for Murder**
    The telephone conversation is not privileged within the meaning of the law.

49. **Unfaded Memory**
    This evidence is sufficient to convict Mario of the offense.

55. **Kidnapping Jenny's Daughter**
    Michael is not guilty.

61. **Choose Your Weapon Carefully**
    Alexander is not guilty.

67. **Mass Produced**
    Avery is not guilty of the offense.

73. **The Lawyer Was Wrong**
    Oliver is entitled to a new trial.

79. **Horse Sense**
    Reginald is not entitled to damages for slander.

85. **Blood Rights**
    The Judge can authorize the transfusion.

4. Cutthroat Law
   The Blakelys did not succeed.

10. The Other Woman
    Mac need not testify about the "other woman."

16. Stabbed and Twice Dropped
    Mildred is guilty.

22. The Employer's Wrath
    The evidence is admissible.

28. Expensive Upgrade
    Cedric can recover only $25,000 from Montgomery.

34. Unwarranted Measures?
    Morton is found guilty.

40. Sealed Bag
    John is guilty.

46. Not Presumed Innocent
    The statement is not sufficient to result in a mistrial.

52. Convenience Store Mugging
    Alice is successful.

58. The Defense of Diligence
    Peter is not guilty.

64. Take the Money and Run
    The widow cannot keep the money.

70. Murder, She Said
    Abigail is guilty of conspiring to commit murder.

76. Water Works
    Pierre can successfully sue Albert.

82. Bad Publicity
    Millie should be successful in her action for defamation.

88. Home Cooking
    The prosecution cannot place in evidence the death of the two sons.

2. A Fig By Any Other Name
   Paul is guilty of assault.

8. Taking the Law Into His Own Hands
   Dean is guilty.

14. The Case of the Slippery Floor
    The defense cannot show this.

20. The Unsuccessful Pickpocket
    Connie is guilty.

26. Armed Robbery
    Leander can be tried and convicted of both offenses.

32. The Tired Lawyer
    Rose's appeal should be allowed.

38. "This *Is* a Constable, Constable"
    Curtis cannot get his money back.

44. Discount Theft?
    Timothy is guilty of theft over $200.

50. You Can Rely on Us
    The bank does not succeed.

56. The Wrong Parts
    Harold is not guilty.

62. Intoxication Plus
    Ralph cannot be convicted of causing death by criminal negligence.

68. Cruise Control
    Pierre is guilty of speeding.

74. The Accompanist
    Glen can recover damages because of the statements in the posters.

80. Fool's Gold
    Duncan can recover damages from Ned.

86. Tennis, Anyone?
    Renee should be allowed to play.

5. Many Are Called—Few Answer
Tim's estate does not recover.

11. The Naked Truth?
The police in no way violated Edmund's privilege against self-incrimination.

17. Buying Votes?
The court did not order a mistrial.

23. Her Husband Did It
The statement is admissible.

29. A Misfire
Alan has to pay despite the common error.

35. Leader of the Pact
Alex is not guilty.

41. Tavern License
The tavern owner's license can be revoked.

47. Double Dose of Cyanide
The evidence of the earlier poisoning is admissible.

53. Policing the Police
The Police Department is guilty of negligence.

59. Too Late for Pistol-Packing
Sally is guilty of attempting to board an aircraft while having a gun in her possession.

65. The Fatal Hostage
They are guilty of murder.

71. Illegal Search?
The evidence is admissible.

77. No Harm, No Foul?
Marcel is not guilty of perjury.

83. Invasion of Privacy?
Val can recover damages for invasion of privacy.

89. Cost Cutting
The law is valid.

3. **Flash Fire**
Harry succeeds.

9. **Pen Pals**
These letters are not admissible in evidence.

15. **Shocking Pictures**
The pictures are admissible.

21. **Fear of Fleeing**
The evidence is admissible.

27. **Speedy Trial**
Roxane cannot be tried again for the same offense.

33. **Child Neglect?**
Isabel is guilty of child neglect.

39. **Off-Duty?**
Richmond is guilty.

45. **Rapid Fire**
The witness can testify as to what Linda told him.

51. **Less Than Meets the Eye**
Jim is guilty of robbery in the first degree.

57. **A Gift of Hacksaw Blades**
Gerrard is guilty.

63. **Practical Joker**
Morris is not guilty.

69. **Once or Forever?**
Daniel is guilty.

75. **Inlaw Outlaw**
Debby's father should be successful.

81. **Sign of the *Times***
Steve was successful.

87. **A Matter of Faith**
Igor should be admitted to the university.

6. **Oh, God!**
   This conversation is not admissible in evidence.

12. **Twice Cruel**
    Natalie can place in evidence the fact that her husband was divorced by a former wife for cruelty.

18. **Serendipity in the Third**
    The evidence is admissible.

24. **Stop the Bus!**
    The statement is admissible.

30. **The Right Charge**
    Eunice is guilty of theft.

36. **Ambulance-Chasing**
    Fabian is not guilty.

42. **Burgled Burglar?**
    The charge should not be dismissed.

48. **The Ends Justify the Means?**
    Jake's confession is admissible.

54. **Unfinished Business**
    They are guilty.

60. **The Joke's On You!**
    Morris is guilty of attempted robbery.

66. **She Never Heard of Henry**
    Kate is guilty.

72. **On-the-Job Training**
    Lloyd's appeal is successful.

78. **The Distracted Mother**
    Mary is responsible in damages for negligent supervision.

84. **The Fatal Trip**
    Abe died by external, violent and accidental means.

90. **The Good News and the Bad News**
    Utility cannot recover from Dr. Smith's insurer.

APPEAL
COURT
DECISIONS

1. The Lady and the Lecher

The hopeful lecher is not guilty of assault, because there was no overt act, no threat, no offer or attempt to injure. He cannot be convicted solely for what may have been in his mind.

State of North Carolina versus Ingram, decided by the Supreme Court of North Carolina, in February, 1953, decision rendered by Judge Armstrong.
Formal legal citation: 74 S.E. (2d) 532

19. A Bad Reference

The evidence is admissible, because the complaints were evidence of knowledge by Otto and his foreman of some defect in Floyd's work.

Borderland Coal Co. versus Kerns, decided by the Court of Appeals of Kentucky, in June, 1915, decision rendered by Judge Hurt.
Formal legal citation: 177 S.W. 266

37. Caution—Inflammable!

Larry's lawsuit is successful, because the warning on the sealer was not explicit enough.

Lambert versus Lastoplex Chemicals Co. Ltd., decided by a panel of five Judges of the Supreme Court of Canada, in December, 1971, decision rendered by Judge Laskin.
Formal legal citation: 25 D.L.R. (3d) 121 (Canada)

55. Kidnapping Jenny's Daughter

Michael is not guilty. To allow prosecution for conspiring to kidnap would frustrate the law's intent, which is to immunize parents from prosecution for kidnapping their own children.

Lythgoe versus the State of Alaska, decided by the Supreme Court of Alaska, in November, 1980, decision rendered by Judge Boochever.
Formal legal citation: 626 P. (2d) 1082

73. The Lawyer Was Wrong

Oliver is entitled to a new trial, because his plea was based on the erroneous advice of his lawyer. Oliver should be allowed to change his plea.

O'Tuel versus Osborne, Attorney General of North Carolina, decided by a panel of three Judges of the United States Court of Appeals, Fourth Circuit, in February, 1983, decision rendered by Judge Sprouse.
Formal legal citation: 706 F. (2d) 498

3. Flash Fire

Harry does not succeed, because the damages were not reasonably foreseeable and were accordingly too remote to justify recovery.

Bradford versus Kanellos, decided by a panel of three Judges of the Ontario Court of Appeal, in December, 1970, decision rendered by Judge Schroeder.

Formal legal citation: [1971] 2 O.R. 393 (Canada)

21. Fear of Fleeing?

The evidence is admissible. Evidence of flight is generally admissible as evidence of guilt, though not necessarily guilt of the crime charged.

State of New Mexico versus Nelson, decided by a panel of five Judges of the Supreme Court of New Mexico, in March, 1959, decision rendered by Judge Compton.

Formal legal citation: 65 N.M. 403

39. Off-Duty?

Richmond is guilty, because the city and the public were obtaining real benefit from the officer's activities. Whether or not the officer was on duty does not matter.

State of New Jersey versus De Santo, decided by a panel of three Judges of the Superior Court of New Jersey, Appellate Division, in December, 1979, decision rendered by Judge Milmed.

Formal legal citation: 410 A. (2d) 704

57. A Gift of Hacksaw Blades

Gerrard is not guilty, since he did not act to put his escape plan into execution. Receipt of the blades was mere preparation.

Smith versus the State of Georgia, decided by a panel of three Judges of the Court of Appeals of Georgia, in October, 1980, decision rendered by Chief Judge Deen.

Formal legal citation: 275 S.E. (2d) 689

75. Inlaw Outlaw

Debby's father should be successful, because the insurance company created a situation of a kind that would have afforded temptation "to a recognizable percentage of humanity to commit murder."

Liberty National Life Insurance Co. versus Weldon, decided by a panel of five Judges of the Supreme Court of Alabama, in November, 1957, decision rendered by Judge Lawson, with Judge Coleman dissenting.

Formal legal citation: 100 So. (2d) 696

2. A Fig By Any Other Name

Paul is guilty of assault because he caused the injury. Force need not be applied directly in order to constitute assault.

Commonwealth (State of Massachusetts) versus Stratton, decided by a panel of the Court of Appeal, in November, 1873, decision rendered by Judge Wells.

Formal legal citation: 19 Am. Rep. 350

20. The Unsuccessful Pickpocket

Connie is guilty. The fact that the theft was impossible is not a defense to a charge of attempt.

R. versus Scott, decided by a panel of three Judges of the Alberta Supreme Court, Appellate Division, in November, 1963, decision rendered by Judge MacDonald.

Formal legal citation: [1964] 2 C.C.C. 257 (Canada)

38. "This *Is* A Constable, Constable"

Curtis cannot get his money back, because contracts cannot be kept open indefinitely; too much time had expired.

Leaf versus International Galleries, decided by a panel of three Judges of the King's Bench Division, in February, 1950, decision rendered by Judge Denning.

Formal legal citation: [1950] 2 K.B. 86 (U.K.)

56. The Wrong Parts

Harold is not guilty, because the prosecution offered no evidence as to what happened to the parts after delivery. That the airline had no use for the parts is insufficient to support a conviction.

State of New Jersey versus Barbossa, decided by a panel of three Judges of the Superior Court of New Jersey, Appellate Division, in December, 1976, decision rendered by the panel, with Judge Seidman dissenting.

Formal legal citation: 384 A. (2d) 523

74. The Accompanist

Glen cannot recover damages because the statements in the posters contained no defamation (that is, no loss of reputation); neither were the words published maliciously.

Shapiro versus La Morta, decided by King's Bench Division, in October, 1923, decision rendered by Judge Lush.

Formal legal citation: 40 T.L.R. 39 (U.K.)

4. Cutthroat Law

The Blakelys did succeed, because Shortal should have anticipated the effect of his act upon the Blakelys.

Blakely versus Shortal, decided by a panel of Judges of the Supreme Court of Iowa, in October, 1945, decision rendered by Justice Mantz.

Formal legal citation: 20 N.W. (2d) 28

22. The Employer's Wrath

The evidence is not admissible. Evidence of measures taken after an incident is not generally admissible.

Turner versus Hearst, decided by a panel of three Judges of the Supreme Court of California, in December, 1896, decision rendered by Judge Henshaw.

Formal legal citation: 47 P. 129

40. Sealed Bag

John is not guilty, because he had made no substantial step towards the commission of the completed offense.

United States versus Joyce, decided by the United States Court of Appeals for the Eighth Circuit, in December, 1982.

Formal legal citation: 32 Cr. L. 2262

58. The Defense of Diligence

Peter is guilty, because the phrase "necessitous circumstances" should be interpreted to accomplish the legislature's intention of compelling spouses to support their children.

State of Kansas versus Knetzer, decided by a panel of three Judges of the Court of Appeals of Kansas, in September, 1979, decision rendered by Judge Abbott.

Formal legal citation: 600 P. (2d) 160

76. Water Works

Pierre can successfully sue Albert, because Albert's negligence was the cause of the low water pressure. Albert's liability is not affected by the city's failure to act.

Gilbert versus New Mexico Construction, decided by a panel of five Judges of the Supreme Court of New Mexico, in February, 1935, decision rendered by Judge Watson, with Judges Hudspeth and Beckley dissenting.

Formal legal citation: 44 P. (2d) 489

5. Many Are Called—Few Answer

Tim's estate does not recover, because there is no duty to rescue at common law.

Osterlind versus Hill, decided by a panel of Judges of the Supreme Judicial Court of Massachusetts, in March, 1928, decision rendered by Judge Braley.

Formal legal citation: 160 N.E. 301

23. Her Husband Did It

The statement is not admissible; it is classic hearsay.

Shepard versus United States of America, decided by the Supreme Court of the United States, in October, 1933, decision rendered by Judge Cardozo.

Formal legal citation: 290 U.S. 96

41. Tavern License

The tavern owner's license can be revoked, because the tavern owner was not a party to the plea negotiations or the subsequent agreement.

Northeast Motor Company, Inc. versus North Carolina State Board of Alcohol Control, decided by a panel of three Judges of the Court of Appeals of North Carolina, in March, 1978, decision rendered by Judge Martin.

Formal legal citation: 241 S.E. (2d) 727

59. Too Late for Pistol-Packing

Sally is guilty of attempting to board an aircraft while having a gun in her possession, because passing through a screening device must be considered an attempt to board the aircraft. The license to carry the gun had no bearing on a charge of attempting to board an aircraft.

The People of the State of Illinois versus Hysner, decided by a panel of three Judges of the Appellate Court of Illinois, First District, Fifth Division, in March, 1978, decision rendered by Justice Mejda.

Formal legal citation: 374 N.E. (2d) 799

77. No Harm, No Foul?

Marcel is guilty of perjury, because whether or not the court is actually misled is irrelevant. Only the intent to mislead is important.

Regina versus Regnier, decided by a panel of three Judges of the Ontario Court of Appeal, in February, 1955, decision rendered by Chief Justice of Ontario Pickup.

Formal legal citation: 21 C.R. 374 (Canada)

7. The Sword or the Scalpel?

Louis is not guilty of murder, because the death was not caused by the stab wound.

R. versus Jordan, decided by a panel of three Judges of the Court of Criminal Appeal, in August, 1956, decision rendered by Judge Hallett.

Formal legal citation: 40 Cr. App. R. 152 (England)

25. Possession of a Firearm

Darlene cannot be charged and convicted of both offenses. They were essentially identical, and it would be unfair if one set of facts could lead to conviction on both charges.

United States versus Girst, decided by the United States Court of Appeals, District of Columbia Circuit, in December, 1979, decision rendered by Judge MacKinnon.

Formal legal citation: F. (2d) 1014

43. Dial M for Murder

The telephone conversation is not privileged within the meaning of the law, because the conversation here showed that no confidentiality was intended, particularly since Herbert knew that the police would be called.

State of South Dakota versus Martin, decided by a panel of two Judges of the Supreme Court of South Dakota, in November, 1978, decision rendered by Judge Miller.

Formal legal citation: 274 N.W. (2d) 893

61. Choose Your Weapon Carefully

Alexander is guilty, since one of the purposes of the law is to protect victims from the fear of physical harm. The word firearm should be given its widest possible meaning.

Holloman versus The Commonwealth of Virginia, decided by a panel of seven Judges of the Supreme Court of Virginia, in August, 1980.

Formal legal citation: 269 S.E. (2d) 356

79. Horse Sense

Reginald is entitled to damages for slander, because the charge of knocking out an eye was an implication of a much greater cruelty than simply beating the horse. Since Nicole could not prove this act of cruelty, she was liable.

Weaver versus Lloyd, decided by the Court of King's Bench, in May, 1824.

Formal legal citation: 107 ER 535 (England)

6. Oh, God!

The conversation is admissible in evidence, because the court decided that, for the purpose of this law, God should not be considered to be a person.

R. versus Davie, decided by the British Columbia County Court, in May, 1979, decision rendered by Judge Lander.
Formal legal citation: 9 C.R. (3d) 275 (Canada)

24. Stop the Bus!

The statement is admissible, because statements made in the heat of the moment are generally admissible.

Schwam versus Reece et al., decided by the Supreme Court of Arkansas, in May, 1948, decision rendered by Justice Millwee.
Formal legal citation: 210 S.W. 903

42. Burgled Burglar?

The charge should be dismissed, because the evidence was lost to the prejudice of Alfredo.

Howard versus the State of Nevada, decided by a panel of five Judges of the Supreme Court of Nevada, in September, 1979, decision rendered by Judge Young.
Formal legal citation: 600 P. (2d) 214

60. The Joke's on You!

Morris is not guilty of attempted robbery, because the evidence was equally consistent with no criminal intent as with intent that was abandoned.

Regina versus Mathe, decided by the British Columbia Court of Appeal, in April, 1973, decision rendered by Judge Maclean.
Formal legal citation: [1973] 4W.W.R. 483 (Canada)

78. The Distracted Mother

Mary is not legally responsible for negligently supervising Kerr, because a parent is not held accountable to her child for careless supervision.

Holodook versus Spencer, decided by the Supreme Court of Columbia County, New York, in January, 1973, decision rendered by Judge A. Franklin Mahoney.
Formal legal citation: 340 N.Y.S. (2d) 311

8. Taking the Law Into His Own Hands

Dean is guilty, because the shot would have caused the death by itself.

State of California versus Lewis, decided by a panel of three Judges of the Supreme Court of California, in May, 1899, decision rendered by Judge Temple.

Formal legal citation: 57 Pac. 470

26. Armed Robbery

Leander cannot be tried and convicted of both offenses, because both offenses require proof of the same facts. Therefore, the facts only support one conviction.

United States versus Hearst, decided by a panel of three Judges of the United States Court of Appeals, Ninth Circuit, in March 1980, decision rendered by Circuit Judge Choy.

Formal legal citation: 638 F. (2d) 1190 (California)

44. Discount Theft?

Timothy is not guilty of theft over $200, because the evidence of value was hearsay. Someone with direct knowledge of the value of the suits should have been called as a witness.

Lee versus State of Arkansas, decided by a panel of three Judges of the Supreme Court of Arkansas, Division 1, in October, 1978.

Formal legal citation: 571 S.W. (2d) 603

62. Intoxication Plus

Ralph cannot be convicted of causing death by criminal negligence, because the blood alcohol level only raises a presumption of intoxication. Such evidence, by itself, is insufficient to prove criminal negligence.

State of Louisiana versus Williams, decided by a panel of four Judges of the Supreme Court of Louisiana, in October, 1977, decision rendered by Justice Marcus, with Judge Dennis dissenting.

Formal legal citation: 354 So. (2d) 152

80. Fool's Gold

Duncan can recover damages from Ned, because Ned's practical joke was premeditated and practised. It directly resulted in damages to Duncan's self-esteem.

Nickerson et al. versus Hodges et al., decided by a panel of three Judges of the Supreme Court of Louisiana, in February, 1920, decision rendered by Judge Dawkins, with Judges Sommerville and O'Neill dissenting.

Formal legal citation: 84 So. 37

9. Pen Pals

These letters are admissible in evidence, because they were not hearsay, but rather evidence of the mental state of the accused.

Sollars versus State of Nevada, decided by the Supreme Court of Nevada, in 1957.

Formal legal citation: 316 P. (2d) 917

27. Speedy Trial

Roxane cannot be tried again for the same offense, because the rule against double jeopardy (being tried twice) applies where there has been a violation of the speedy trial rule.

State of Indiana versus Roberts, decided by a panel of three Judges of the Court of Appeals of Indiana, in December, 1976, decision rendered by Chief Judge Robertson.

Formal legal citation: 358 N.E. (2d) 181

45. Rapid Fire

The witness can testify as to what Linda told him, because Linda's statement was a spontaneous utterance, made in response to a startling incident, without opportunity for reflection and fabrication.

State of North Carolina versus Johnson, decided by the Supreme Court of North Carolina, in January, 1978, decision rendered by Judge Copeland.

Formal legal citation: 239 S.E. (2d) 806

63. Practical Joker

Morris is guilty, because he should have foreseen the risk of injury. His behavior was a gross deviation from the standard of care that an ordinary person would have exercised.

State of Utah versus Hallett and Felsch, decided by a panel of four Judges of the Supreme Court of Utah, in October, 1980, decision rendered by Chief Justice Crockett.

Formal legal citation: 619 P. (2d) 335

81. Sign of the *Times*

Steve was not successful, because criticism of public officials in their capacity as such is sanctioned by the constitution, unless such criticism is false and motivated by actual malice. There was no proof of actual malice here and no defamation action can be taken.

New York Times Company versus Sullivan, decided by a panel of six Judges of the United States Supreme Court, in January, 1964, decision rendered by Judge Brennan.

Formal legal citation: 376. U.S. 254

11. The Naked Truth?

The police in no way violated Edmund's privilege against self-incrimination.

Schmerber versus State of California, decided by a panel of nine Judges of the United States Supreme Court, in April, 1966, decision rendered by Judge Brennan representing the opinions of five judges, with dissenting opinions rendered by Judges Warren, Black, Douglas, Fortas.

Formal legal citation: 384 U.S. 757

29. A Misfire

Alan has to pay despite the common error, because Alan got what he had asked for under the contract. His misunderstanding does not relieve him from the obligation to pay.

Upton-on-Severn Rural District Council versus Powell, decided by a panel of three Judges of the Court of Appeal, in January, 1942, decision rendered by Lord Greene.

Formal legal citation: [1942] 1 All E.R. 220 (England)

47. Double Dose of Cyanide

The evidence is not admissible, because no connection was shown between Henry and the first wife's poisoning.

Noor Mohamed versus The King, decided by a panel of five Judges of the Judicial Committee of the Privy Council in November, 1949, decision rendered by Lord Uthwatt.

Formal legal citation: [1949] A.C. 182 (U.K.)

65. The Fatal Hostage

They are guilty of murder, because the death of Caroline would not have occurred had Steve and Tim not committed the robbery.

Jackson and Wells Jr. versus the State of Maryland, decided by a panel of seven Judges of the Court of Appeals of Maryland, in December, 1979, decision rendered by Judge Orth.

Formal legal citation: 408 A. (2d) 711

83. Invasion of Privacy?

Val cannot recover damages because there was no "publicity" here. Only Val's relatives and employer were contacted, and such a small group does not satisfy the requirement of publicity.

Vogel Jr. and Smith versus W.T. Grant Company, decided by a panel of two Judges of the Supreme Court of Pennsylvania, in October, 1974, decision rendered by Judge Manderino.

Formal legal citation: 327 A. (2d) 133

10. The Other Woman

Mac must testify about the "other woman," because he is seeking judgment in his favor. He must therefore subject himself to cross-examination.

Nuckols versus Nuckols, decided by a panel of three Judges of the District Court of Appeal of Florida, in September, 1966, decision rendered by Judge Lopez.

Formal legal citation: 189 So. (2d) 832

28. Expensive Upgrade

Cedric can recover $100,000 from Montgomery, because Cedric is entitled to the land at a uniform grade, even if the cost is disproportionate to the value of the land.

Groves versus Wunder, decided by a panel of two Judges of the Supreme Court of Minnesota, in April, 1939, decision rendered by Justice Stone.

Formal legal citation: 286 N.W. 235

46. Not Presumed Innocent

The statement is not sufficient to result in a mistrial. It was nothing more than an explanation to the jury of its right to find the defendant guilty.

The People of the State of Illinois versus Mathews, decided by a panel of three Judges of the Appellate Court of Illinois, Third District, in February, 1979, decision rendered by Judge Stengel.

Formal legal citation: 387 N.E. (2d) 10

64. Take the Money and Run

The widow cannot keep the money, because money paid under a mistake of fact can generally be recovered.

Kelly versus Solari, decided by the U.K. Court of Exchequer, in November, 1841.

Formal legal citation: 152 E.R. 24 (U.K.)

82. Bad Publicity

Millie should be successful in her action for defamation, because Millie was not a public figure. She did not assume any role of special prominence in the affairs of society nor did she "thrust herself to the forefront of any particular controversy in order to influence the resolution of the issues involved in it."

Time, Inc. versus Firestone, decided by a panel of four Judges of the United States Supreme Court, in October, 1975, decision rendered by Judges Powell, Brennan, White and Marshall.

Formal legal citation: 424 U.S. 448

12. Twice Cruel

Natalie cannot place this in evidence. Evidence of a party's bad character is not generally admissible.

Bosworth versus Bosworth, decided by the Supreme Court of Errors of Connecticut, in November, 1944, decision rendered by Judge Dickinson.

Formal legal citation: 40 A. (2d) 186

30. The Right Charge

Eunice is not guilty of theft, because there was a contract of sale. She was therefore guilty of fraud, not theft.

Regina versus Dawood, decided by a panel of three Judges of the Alberta Supreme Court, Appellate Division, in September, 1975, decision rendered by Judge McDermid, with Judge Clement dissenting.

Formal legal citation: [1976] 1 W.W.R. 262 (Canada)

48. The Ends Justify the Means?

Jake's confession is admissible, because force was applied to discover the girl's location and not to extract a confession. The violence did not taint the confession.

Leon versus State of Florida, decided by a panel of Judges of the Florida Court of Appeal, Third District, in February, 1982, with Judge Ferguson dissenting.

Formal legal citation: 31 Cr. L. 2038

66. She Never Heard of Henry

Kate is not guilty, because her answer in no way interrupted the police's progress towards their objective.

The State of Ohio versus Stephens, decided by a panel of three Judges of the Court of Appeals of Ohio, Hamilton County, in July, 1978.

Formal legal citation: 387 N.E. (2d) 252

84. The Fatal Trip

Abe died by "external, violent and accidental means," within the meaning of the insurance policy, because the fall was the immediate cause of death. This fall was properly characterized as an accident.

Moran versus Massachusetts Mutual Life Insurance Co., decided by a panel of three Judges of the Supreme Court, Appellate Term, First Department, in June, 1941.

Formal legal citation: 29 N.Y.S. (2d) 33

13. The Belligerent Victim

The evidence is admissible, because a victim's reputation for violence is generally admissible.

Freeman versus State of Mississippi, decided by a panel of four Judges of the Supreme Court of Mississippi, in December, 1967. *Formal legal citation: 204 So. (2d) 842*

31. Hair Today and Tomorrow

Shirley won, because the advertisement was an offer. Shirley accepted the offer. There was a contract.

Goldthorpe versus Logan, decided by a panel of three Judges of the Ontario Court of Appeal, in March, 1943, decision rendered by Judge Laidlaw. *Formal legal citation: [1943] O.W.N. 215 (Canada)*

49. Unfaded Memory

The evidence is sufficient to convict Mario of the offense, even though the identification was made out of court. A jury could find Mario guilty beyond a reasonable doubt.

Bedford versus State of Maryland, decided by a panel of seven Judges of the Maryland Court of Appeals, in March, 1982, with three Judges dissenting. *Formal legal citation: 31 Cr. L. 2056*

67. Mass Produced

Avery is not guilty of the offense, because the language of the law does not apply to modern commercially manufactured products, such as brand-name watches.

The People of the State of New York versus James, decided by the District Court, Nassau County, First District, Criminal Part 1, in October, 1974, decision rendered by Judge Ralph Diamond. *Formal legal citation: 361 N.Y.S. (2d) 255*

85. Blood Rights

The judge can authorize the transfusion, because the state has an interest in the conservation of life. The hospital authorities should be allowed to exercise medical judgment in the face of the parents' refusal.

John F. Kennedy Memorial Hospital versus Heston and Heston, decided by a panel of six Judges of the Supreme Court of New Jersey, in February, 1971, decision rendered by Judge Weintraub. *Formal legal citation: 279 A. (2d) 670*

16. Stabbed and Twice Dropped

Mildred is guilty, because the stab wound was a contributing factor in the death.

R. versus Smith, decided by the Courts-Martial Appeal Court, in March, 1959, decision rendered by The Lord Chief Justice, Mr. Justice Streatfield.

Formal legal citation: 43 Cr. App. R. 121 (England)

34. Unwarranted Measures?

Morton is found guilty, because the police didn't rely on the arrest warrant to make the arrest. The ruse did not violate the accused's constitutional rights.

State of Washington versus Myers, decided by the Washington Court of Appeals, in August, 1983.

Formal legal citation: 33 Cr. L. 2505

52. Convenience Store Mugging

Alice is successful, because it is the store owner's duty to his customers to take reasonable care in providing a safe place at which to shop.

Butler versus Acme Markets Inc., decided by the New Jersey Supreme Court, in May, 1982.

Formal legal citation: 31 Cr. L. 2222

70. Murder, She Said

Abigail is guilty of conspiring to commit murder, because her trip and discussions with the police officer were an overt act made in furtherance of the plan to kill her rival.

Blaylock versus the State of Oklahoma, decided by a panel of three Judges of the Court of Criminal Appeals of Oklahoma, in July, 1979, decision rendered by Judge Bussey.

Formal legal citation: 598 P. (2d) 251

88. Home Cooking

The prosecution can place in evidence the deaths of the two sons, because Cynthia prepared the food and she alone did not suffer from arsenic poisoning.

Regina versus Geering, decided by a panel of three Judges of a U.K. Court, in August, 1849.

Formal legal citation: 18 L.J. MC. 215 (U.K.)

14. The Case of the Slippery Floor

The defense may show this, because the evidence was so extensive as to justify an inference of a history of safety.

Erickson versus Walgreen Drug Co. et al., decided by a panel of three Judges of the Supreme Court of Utah, in June, 1951, decision rendered by Judge Wolfe.

Formal legal citation: 232 P (2d) 210

32. The Tired Lawyer

Rose's appeal should be allowed, because a sleeping lawyer is the same as no lawyer at all. Actual prejudice need not be shown.

Javor versus United States, decided by a panel of Judges of the United States Court of Appeals for the Ninth Circuit, in January, 1984, with Judge Anderson dissenting.

Formal legal citation: 34 Cr. L. 2375

50. You Can Rely on Us

The bank succeeds, because accountants are liable to any person who might reasonably be expected to rely on their statements.

Haig versus Bamford, decided by a panel of nine Judges of the Supreme Court of Canada, in April, 1976.

Formal legal citation: [1977] 1 S.C.R. 466 (Canada)

68. Cruise Control

Pierre is guilty of speeding, because by delegating partial control of his car through the use of the speed control, Pierre was the agent who caused the act of speeding.

State of Kansas versus Baker, decided by a panel of three Judges of the Court of Appeals of Kansas, in August, 1977, decision rendered by Judge Spencer.

Formal legal citation: 571 P. (2d) 65

86. Tennis, Anyone?

Renee should be allowed to play, because the chromosome test is unfair, discriminatory and inequitable; it concentrates on only one factor in ascertaining sex and does not allow consideration of other factors.

Richards versus United States Tennis Association, U.S. Open Tennis Championship Committee and Women's Tennis Association, Inc., decided by the Supreme Court, Special Term, New York County, Part 1, in August, 1977, decision rendered by Judge Alfred Ascione.

Formal legal citation: 400 N.Y.S. 2d 267

17. Buying Votes?

The court ordered a mistrial, because it is improper to allow a jury and a party to a trial to fraternize.

Scott versus Tubbs, decided by a panel of three Judges of the Supreme Court of Colorado, in April, 1908, decision rendered by Judge Steele.

Formal legal citation: 95 P. 540

35. Leader of the Pact

Alex is not guilty, because this was really a double attempted suicide. At most he would be guilty of aiding and abetting a suicide.

Forden versus Joseph G., decided by the California Supreme Court, in August, 1983.

Formal legal citation: 33 Cr. L. 2511

53. Policing the Police

The Police Department is guilty of negligence, because it was reasonably foreseeable that an officer unfit to carry a gun might injure members of his family.

Bonsignore versus City of New York, decided by the United States Court of Appeals for the Second Circuit, in June, 1982.

Formal legal citation: 31 Cr. L. 2294

71. Illegal Search?

The evidence is admissible, because searches of open fields do not violate any reasonable expectation of privacy.

United States of America versus Oliver, decided by a panel of five Judges of the United States Court of Appeals, Sixth Circuit, in February, 1982, decision rendered by Judge Bailey Brown, and Judges Keith, Edwards Jr., Lively and Jones dissenting.

Formal legal citation: 686 F. (2d) 356

89. Cost Cutting

The law is invalid, because it arbitrarily discriminates against the most seriously injured victims of medical malpractice.

Wright versus Central Du Page Hospital Association, decided by a panel of three Judges of the Supreme Court of Illinois, in May, 1976, decision rendered by Judge Goldenhersh and Judges Underwood and Ryan partially dissenting.

Formal legal citation: 347 N.E. (2d) 736

15. Shocking Pictures

The pictures are admissible, because direct evidence of injuries is generally admissible, notwithstanding its effect upon the jury.

People of the State of California versus Kemp, decided by a panel of Judges of the Supreme Court of California, in January, 1974, with Judge McComb dissenting.

Formal legal citation: 517 P. (2d) 826

33. Child Neglect?

Isabel is not guilty of child neglect, because there was no recognized or recognizable dangerous condition in Isabel's house from which substantial and unjustifiable risk could be inferred.

State of Oregon versus Goff, decided by a panel of Judges of the Oregon Court of Appeals, in January, 1984, with three Judges dissenting.

Formal legal citation: 34 Cr. L. 2409

51. Less Than Meets the Eye

Jim is not guilty of robbery in the first degree, because the language of the law leads to the inescapable conclusion that actual possession of a weapon is a requirement for a conviction.

State of New Jersey versus Butler, decided by a panel of Judges of the New Jersey Supreme Court, in May, 1982, with two Judges dissenting.

Formal legal citation: 31 Cr. L. 2220

69. Once or Forever?

Daniel is not guilty, because the crime was committed when Daniel accepted the coat. Mere possession of the coat was not a continuing crime.

Duncan versus the State of Maryland, decided by a panel of two Judges of the Court of Appeals of Maryland, in April, 1978, decision rendered by Judge Orth and concurring decision rendered by Chief Judge Murphy.

Formal legal citation: 384 A. (2d) 456

87. A Matter of Faith

Igor should be admitted to the university, because it did not require vaccination of Christian Scientists. To exclude Igor would be to show preference for one set of religious beliefs over another.

Kolbeck versus Kramer and Rutgers, The State University, decided by a panel of seven Judges of the Supreme Court of New Jersey, in October, 1965.

Formal legal citation: 214 A. (2d) 408

18. Serendipity in the Third

The evidence is admissible, because evidence can be admitted to show that the establishment was a bookie joint. It would violate the hearsay rule only if it were admitted to show that the caller's words were true.

State of Connecticut versus Tolisano, decided by a panel of five Judges of the Supreme Court of Errors of Connecticut, in November, 1949, decision rendered by Judge Jennings.

Formal legal citation: 70 A. (2d) 118

36. Ambulance-Chasing

Fabian is not guilty, because the statute is too broad; for example, it might prohibit a friend who was a lawyer from advising an injured victim.

People of the State of Michigan versus Posner, decided by the Court of Appeals of Michigan, in October, 1977, decision rendered by Judge Kaufman.

Formal legal citation: 261 N.W. (2d) 209

54. Unfinished Business

They are not guilty, because there was no actual entry into the store. The most they could have been convicted of was an attempt to break and enter.

Stamps versus Commonwealth of Kentucky, decided by a panel of six Judges of the Supreme Court of Kentucky, in July, 1980.

Formal legal citation: 602 S.W. (2d) 172

72. On-the-Job Training

Lloyd's appeal is not successful, because actual errors in handling the case must be demonstrated before reversal will be granted.

United States of America versus Cronic, decided by a panel of two Judges of the United States Supreme Court, in January, 1984, decision rendered by Judge Stevens.

Formal legal citation: 104 Sct. 2039

90. The Good News and the Bad News

Utility cannot recover from Dr. Smith's insurer, because Utility's claim against Dr. Smith, whom it employed, was not for malpractice but rather for breach of contract or fraud.

McFarling versus Azar, decided by a panel of three Judges of the United States Court of Appeal, Fifth Circuit, in September, 1975, decision rendered by Judge Golbold.

Formal legal citation: 519 F. (2d) 1075 (Fla)

RULES OF THE GAME

With two or more, you can play this book as a game. The rules are simple:

Player #1 reads the facts of a case and tries to figure out the trial court decision. If it is correct, Player #1 gets one point. The other players are free to appeal that decision.

A price must be paid, however, for the right to appeal: three points. (In this game, as in real life, justice is not cheap.)

If the appealing player or players are unsuccessful, they simply lose the three points. If they are successful, however, each receives four points and Player #1 loses two points.

If Player #1 is incorrect in predicting the trial decision, he loses one point. Only he has the right to appeal that finding. He too must pay three points in order to exercise his right of appeal.

If he is incorrect on appeal, he will have lost four points total. If he is successful on appeal, he wins five points. In other words, a player who is wrong at trial but who wins on appeal gains one point in the process.

* * * * * * * *

To summarize, here are the possible results for Player #1 after a case has been completed:

- a gain of one point if he correctly predicts the trial outcome and is not challenged—or if he is challenged and the decision is upheld on appeal.
- a loss of one point of he correctly predicts the trial outcome but the trial decision is reversed on appeal.
- a loss of one point if he incorrectly predicts the trial outcome and chooses not to appeal.
- a loss of four points if he incorrectly predicts the trial outcome and unsuccessfully appeals.

The following are the possible results for a player who chooses to appeal a correct finding by Player #1:

- a gain of one point if the appeal is successful.
- a loss of three points if the appeal is unsuccessful.

The players take turns reading the cases. The game ends when one player reaches ten points. Scores can go negative, and don't be surprised if this happens quite often, until players recognize the true cost of litigation.

INDEX